JS

The Leopard and the Sky God

Retold by Mairi Mackinnon

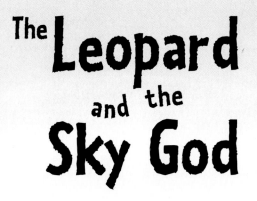

Illustrated by
Ali Lodge

Reading Consultant: Alison Kelly
Roehampton University

This story is about

the Sky God,

the
leopard,

his drum,

2

the python,

the elephant

and the
tortoise.

Long ago, when the world
was new,

the animals
lived in the forest.

High up above lived
the Sky God.

One day, the Sky God
heard a wonderful sound.

He leaned down and
looked through the trees.

There was the leopard,
playing a great big drum.

Wow!

He played *high*

and **low.**

He played *soft*

and **loud!**

"Hello, Leopard," said the Sky God.

"That's a fine drum.
May I try it?"

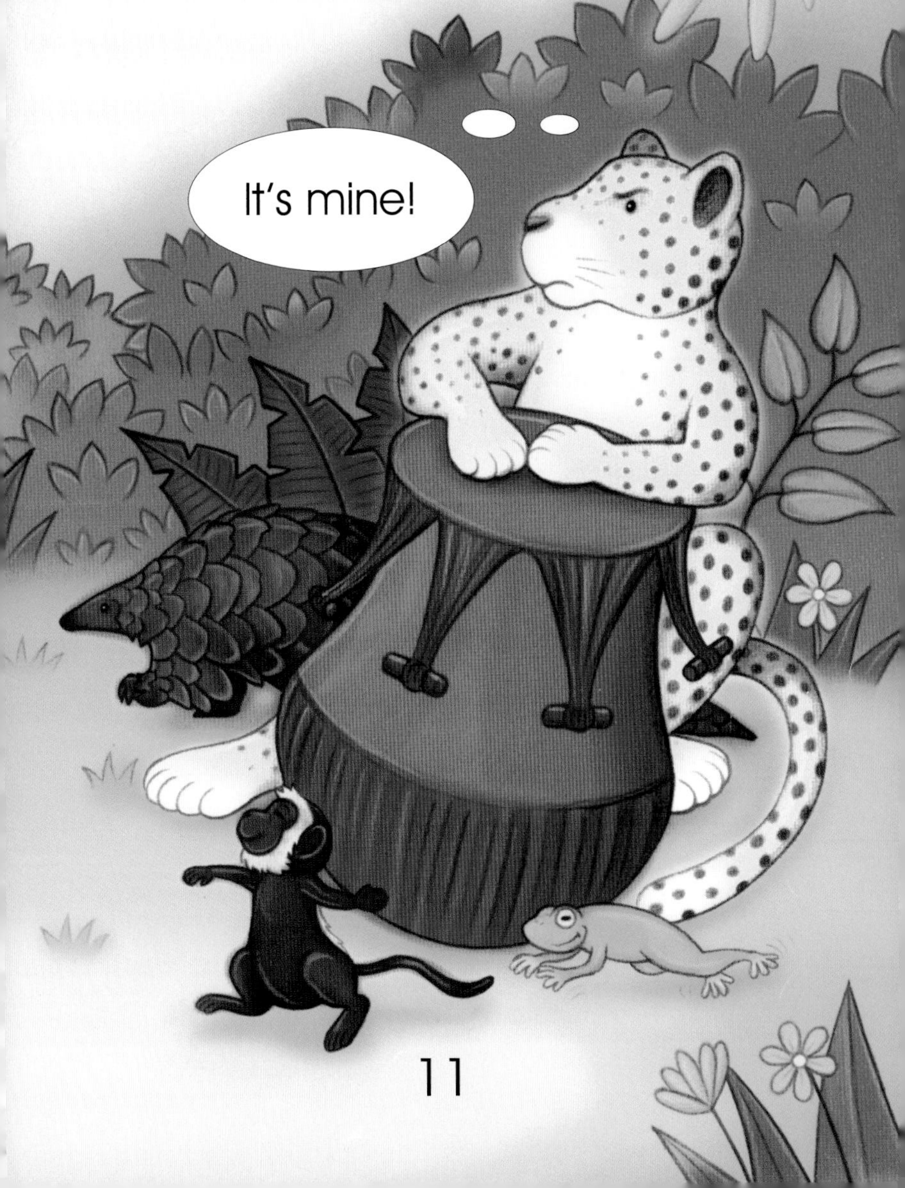

"Sorry," said the leopard.
He shook his head.

"I'll be very careful," said
the Sky God.

Come on,
share it.

"No," said the leopard.

The Sky God waited.

I'll borrow it when he goes hunting.

But the leopard kept his
eye on the drum the
whole time.

The Sky God walked away.
"What's the matter?"
asked the other animals.

Leopard won't let
me play his drum.

"I wish I had that drum,"
the Sky God said.

"I'll talk to Leopard,"
said the python.

He found the leopard,
playing his drum as usual.

"What do you want?"
growled the leopard.

"May I look at your drum?" asked the python.

"No!" roared the leopard,

Go away!

and he showed his long
teeth and his sharp claws.

The python slithered
away quickly.

"Well?" said the Sky God.
"Sorry," said the python.

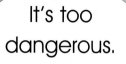

It's too dangerous.

"I'm not scared," said the elephant. "I'll talk to him."

He soon heard the drum.
Where was the leopard?

The elephant looked
around. There he was –
up in a tree.

"May I look at
your drum?" asked
the elephant.

"Leave me alone!"
roared the leopard.

27

The elephant shook and
shook the tree...

...but he couldn't shake
the leopard out.

"Well?" said the Sky God.
"Sorry," said the elephant.

It's too difficult.

"Let me try,"
said the tortoise.

29

Now in those days the tortoise had no shell, only a little soft body.

You?

The others laughed.
"You'll never do it."

But the tortoise said,
"Wait and see."

31

She found the leopard
in his tree.

Mr. Leopard!
Mr. Leopard!

"Have you seen the Sky God's drum?" she asked.

Whose drum?

"The Sky God doesn't have a drum," said the leopard.

Oh yes he does.

"It's enormous," said
the tortoise. "He can
climb inside it."

35

The leopard climbed
down from the tree.

He rolled the drum
along the ground and
crawled inside.

Like this?

"Right inside,"
said the tortoise.

Then she looked around and spotted the leopard's cooking pot.

Quickly, she clapped
the lid over the end of
the drum.

Then she rolled it along
to the Sky God.

The Sky God was very pleased.

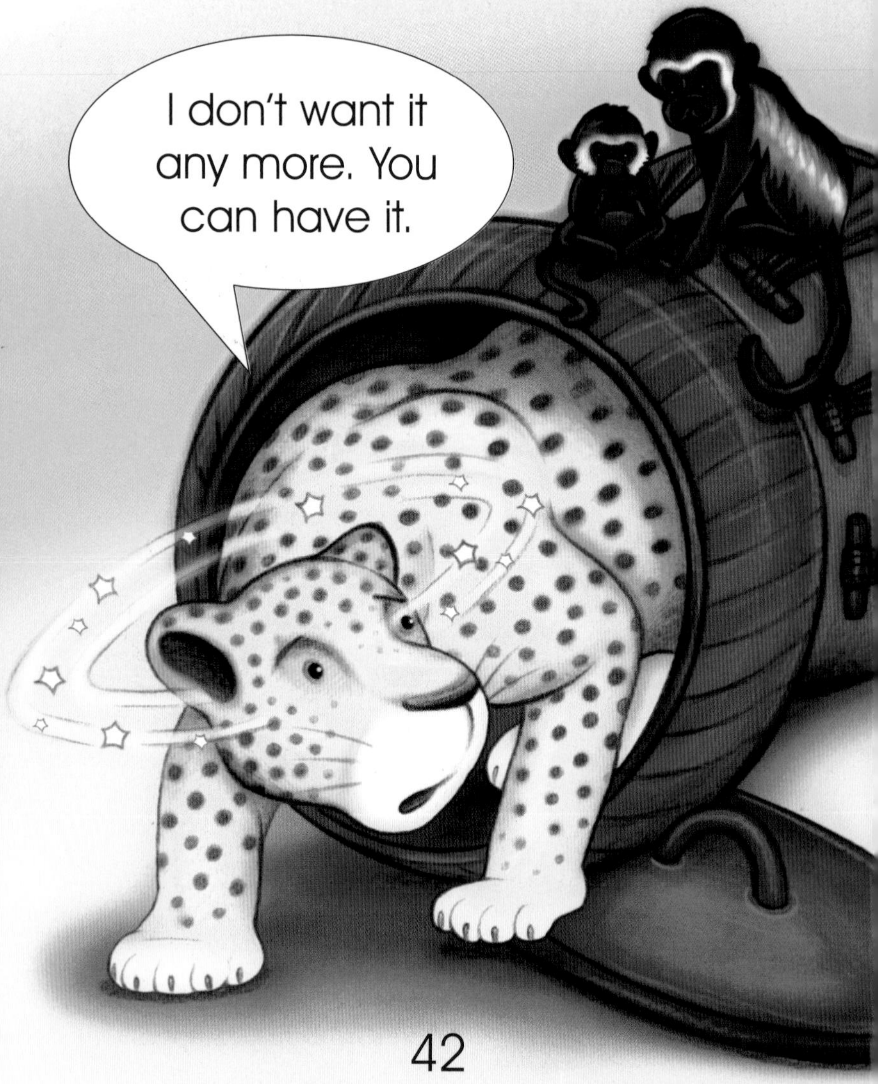

Then the tortoise said,
"Sky God, can you do
something for me?"

43

She looked at the drum.
"I would like a shell on
my body...

...so that nothing can hurt me."

"Yes, of course," said the Sky God.

The Sky God loved his drum.

And, when the weather is stormy, you can still hear him...

playing high and low,

playing *soft* and **loud!**

The Leopard and the Sky God is a very
old story from the Asante kingdom in
West Africa (now in the country of Ghana).

Series editor
Lesley Sims

Designed by
Catherine-Anne MacKinnon

First published in 2007 by Usborne Publishing Ltd., Usborne House,
83-85 Saffron Hill, London EC1N 8RT, England. www.usborne.com
Copyright © 2007 Usborne Publishing Ltd.

48